EGYPTIAN CURSE

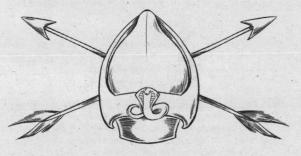

First published in Great Britain by HarperCollins *Children's Books* in 2014
HarperCollins *Children's Books* is a division of HarperCollins*Publishers* Ltd,
1 London Bridge Street, London SE1 9GF

The HarperCollins website address is: www.harpercollins.co.uk

6

Text © Hothouse Fiction Limited, 2014
Illustrations © HarperCollins *Children's Books*, 2014
Illustrations by Dynamo

ISBN 978-0-00-751408-3

Printed and bound by CPI Group (UK) Ltd, Croydon, CR0 4YY

MIX
Paper from
responsible sources
FSC™ C007454

FSC™ is a non-profit international organisation established to promote
the responsible management of the world's forests. Products carrying the
FSC label are independently certified to assure consumers that they come
from forests that are managed to meet the social, economic and
ecological needs of present and future generations,
and other controlled sources.

Find out more about HarperCollins and the environment at
www.harpercollins.co.uk/green

CHRIS BLAKE

TiME HUNTERS

EGYPTIAN CURSE

HarperCollins *Children's Books*

Travel through time with Tom
on more

adventures!

Gladiator Clash

Knight Quest

Viking Raiders

Greek Warriors

Pirate Mutiny

Egyptian Curse

Cowboy Showdown

Samurai Assassin

Outback Outlaw

Stone Age Rampage

Mohican Brave

Aztec Attack

For games, competitions and more visit:

www.time-hunters.com

CONTENTS

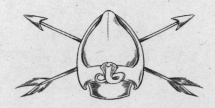

With special thanks to
Marnie Stanton-Riches

PROLOGUE

Five thousand years ago

Princess Isis and her pet cat, Cleo, stood outside the towering carved gates to the Afterlife. It had been rotten luck to fall off a pyramid and die at only ten years of age, but Isis wasn't worried – the Afterlife was meant to be great. People were dying to go there, after all! Her mummy's wrappings were so uncomfortable she couldn't wait a second longer to get in, get her body back and wear normal clothes again.

"Oi, Aaanuuubis, Anubidooby!" Isis shouted impatiently. "When you're ready, you old dog!"

Cleo started to claw Isis's shoulder. Then she yowled, jumping from Isis's arms and cowering behind her legs.

"Calm down, fluffpot," Isis said, bending to stroke her pet. "He can't exactly woof me to death!" The princess laughed, but froze when she stood up. Now she understood what Cleo had been trying to tell her.

Looming up in front of her was the enormous jackal-headed god of the Underworld himself, Anubis. He was so tall that Isis's neck hurt to look up at him. He glared down his long snout at her with angry red eyes. There was nothing pet-like about him. Isis gulped.

"'WHEN YOU'RE READY, YOU OLD DOG?'" Anubis growled. "'ANUBIDOOBY?'"

Isis gave the god of the Underworld a winning smile and held out five shining amulets. She had been buried with them so she could give them to Anubis to gain entry to the Afterlife. There was a sixth amulet too – a gorgeous green one. But Isis had hidden it under her arm. Green *was* her favourite colour, and surely Anubis didn't need all six.

Except the god didn't seem to agree. His fur bristled in rage. "FIVE? Where is the sixth?" he demanded.

Isis shook her head. "I was only given five," she said innocently.

To her horror, Anubis grabbed the green amulet from its hiding place. "You little LIAR!" he bellowed.

Thunder started to rumble. The ground shook. Anubis snatched all six amulets and tossed them into the air. With a loud crack and a flash of lightning, they vanished.

"You hid them from me!" he boomed. "Now I have hidden them from you – in the most dangerous places throughout time."

Isis's bandaged shoulders drooped in despair. "So I c-c-can't come into the Afterlife then?"

"Not until you have found each and every

10

one. But first, you will have to get out of this…" Anubis clicked his fingers. A life-sized pottery statue of the goddess Isis, whom Isis was named after, appeared before him.

Isis felt herself being sucked into the statue, along with Cleo. "What are you doing to me?" she yelled.

"You can only escape if somebody breaks the statue," Anubis said. "So you'll have plenty of time to think about whether trying to trick the trickster god himself was a good idea!"

The walls of the statue closed around Isis, trapping her and Cleo inside. The sound of Anubis's evil laughter would be the last sound they would hear for a long, long time…

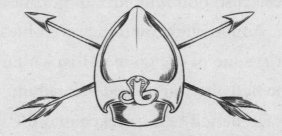

CHAPTER 1
BOWLED OVER

"Wakey-wakey, Tom!" called Mum from downstairs. "You don't want to sleep through your party!"

The smell of frying bacon wafted under Tom's bedroom door and interrupted his dream about playing football with a gang of pirates on a Caribbean beach.

He opened his eyes and tried to work out why he felt so excited.

"Oh, yeah!" he said, suddenly remembering.

Tom sprang out of bed and shook the
bandaged figure sleeping on the floor.

"Wake up, Isis! It's my birthday!" he said.

"Ow!" Isis cried. With her arms folded
over her chest, mummified Princess Isis
Amun-Ra sat up stiffly. "That's *not* a nice
way to be woken up!" she said. There was
a creak as she stretched her arms. A cloud of
dust swirled round her.

"Sorry! I'm just excited," Tom said, as he helped Isis to her feet.

"OK, but a girl needs her beauty sleep, you know," Isis snapped.

Tom chuckled. "You're an Ancient Egyptian mummy. Even the longest sleep won't bring you back to life!"

He went over to his dressing gown and slippers, which lay in a heap on the floor. Cleopatra, Isis's mummified pet cat, was snoozing on top of them.

"Up you get, Cleo!" Tom said. Then, turning to Isis, Tom explained, "Mum always cooks me a special birthday breakfast. I'll have sausage, bacon, egg, mushrooms and beans waiting for me downstairs."

"Birthday this! Birthday that! What's so great about a birthday?" Isis muttered, as she scooped Cleo into her arms.

"Er, it's only the best day of the year, silly!" Tom cried. Then he looked at his friend and frowned. "Hang on – did you celebrate birthdays in Ancient Egypt?" he asked. "You know — get presents, eat cake, have a party..."

Isis shook her head stiffly. "When I was alive, we used to have a party to celebrate the goddess Isis. And because I'm named after her, everybody made a fuss of me. Now *that* was fun!"

Tom pulled on his dressing gown and did a little dance. "I was born eleven years ago today! How cool is that?"

"Not very. I was born five thousand years ago," Isis said smugly.

Ignoring her, Tom thought about the things he had put on his birthday list.

"Hey, I wonder if I'll get *Timeline of Fire*?

15

The computer game where you get to fight historical battles."

"What a silly thing to ask for!" Isis said, sitting on Tom's bed. "You should have asked for jewels or a gold statue of yourself."

Tom slid his feet inside his slippers. "The only jewel I want," he said, "is the sixth amulet, so I don't have to share a bedroom with you any more, Your Royal Crustiness."

Isis stood up and shuffled over to Tom's desk, where his books were lined up. She pushed over a large history encyclopedia at one end and the rest of the books toppled over like dominos.

"Until you met me, Professor Smartypants, all you had for excitement were these dusty books," she said. "I've shown you what it's like to have some *real* adventures! You should be kissing my feet."

Tom looked down at Isis's flaky yellow toes. "Ugh. No thanks."

"*You* broke that statue in your dad's museum," she continued. "Me and Cleo had been quite happy there until you came along."

Tom groaned. "No, you weren't! And *you're* the one who got into trouble with Anubis in the first place. *You* got yourself banished from the Afterlife until you can find all six amulets. So it's *your* fault we've both had to risk life and limb—"

"*I* haven't risked my life. I'm already dead. Or hadn't you noticed?" Isis pointed at her bandaged chest. "But the fact *you're* still alive, despite facing up to Roman gladiators, medieval knights, raiding Vikings, Greek warriors and crazy pirates, is completely down to me!"

Cleo purred and stretched her legs stiffly.

"See!" Isis said. "Even Cleo agrees, don't you, my fluffy love?"

Tom started putting his books back on the desk. He knew by now there was no point in arguing with Isis.

"Happy birthday, darling!" Mum said, sliding Tom's breakfast on to the kitchen table and giving him a kiss.

Dad pushed his glasses up his nose. "I can't believe you're eleven! Seems like only yesterday you were in nappies."

Isis giggled and Tom shot her a warning look.

Dad clapped Tom on the arm. "Ready for your presents?"

"You bet," Tom said, shovelling a forkful of beans into his mouth and then tearing at the wrapping paper. He pulled out a chunky red-and-green jumper covered in... *What is it covered in?* Tom thought, staring at the yellow markings on the chest.

"Are those supposed to be hieroglyphics?" Isis asked. She was sitting on the kitchen worktop, but Tom's mum and dad couldn't see or hear her.

"One arm's shorter than the other," Tom said.

"The jumper's from Nan," Mum explained, and then handed Tom another present. "From me," she said, smiling.

Tom felt the package. It was square and hard. "Computer game?" he guessed correctly, unwrapping *Timeline of Fire.* "Yesssss!"

Then Dad plonked something large and heavy on the kitchen table. He cleared his throat. "And this is from me."

Tom unwrapped the gift. "The *Young Historian* books box set!" Tom yelled. "Wicked! Look, it's got an Aztec Empire special edition too." He grinned at his parents. "Thanks, Mum and Dad, you're the best!"

As Tom gobbled up his fried egg, Isis's
voice floated over the room.

"A computer game, some books and a
knitted thing? What boring presents!"

Tom noticed that Isis's shoulders were
slumped. Perhaps she was feeling left
out, especially if she'd never celebrated a
birthday before. He quickly ate the rest of his
breakfast. "Let's go upstairs and try out my
new game," he whispered.

"Deal!" Isis said, smiling.

As they ran upstairs, Mum shouted out,
"Don't forget we're leaving for the bowling
alley at ten thirty!"

"Those shoes are ugly," Isis said, pointing
to the red, white and blue bowling shoes
that Tom and his friends were putting
on.

"Nobody's asking *you* to wear them," Tom said.

Mum and Dad were programming everybody's names into the machine that kept score.

In the next lane, a tall man stood up to take his go. Tom watched as the ball thundered down the lane. There was a loud crash as it sent every single pin flying. The man jumped up and down and punched the air.

Isis gasped. "That's not very sporting, is it?"

Tom started to laugh. "He got a strike," he explained. "He's happy because he knocked down all the pins. That's the point of the game, you see? The more you knock down—"

"I bet I can do that!" Isis said.

Tom nervously glanced over at his friends.

"No, Isis. Just watch. Please don't try to join in—"

But Isis had already picked up a bowling ball and flung it down the lane.

"Woo-hoo!" she cried, as Cleo scampered after the ball.

Tom's friends stared as, seemingly on its own, the ball rolled down the lane and knocked over all ten pins.

"That ball just bowled a strike by itself!" Veejay said, blinking in disbelief.

Tom gulped. "Someone must have dropped it." To distract his friends he said, "Hey! Who wants some lemonade?"

Suddenly, Tom's voice was drowned out by a loud, rumbling noise. At the end of the lane, the giant, jackal-headed god of the Underworld, Anubis, burst out, splintering the wood and sending the pins flying.

"Just when I was getting the hang of it!"
Isis grumbled.

Anubis's eyes glowed red. He folded his
arms and bared his sharp teeth at Tom and

Isis. "Are you ready to face your toughest challenge yet?" he boomed.

Tom looked at his school friends who were all sipping their lemonade. They had no idea the Ancient Egyptian god was there.

"Not really," Tom said. "I'm in the middle of my birthday party."

"SILENCE!" bellowed Anubis. "Your last challenge will be a real test of bravery. Fail, and Isis will *never* get into the Afterlife!"

Suddenly, a wind blew up round Tom, Isis and Cleo, pulling them out of the bowling alley and into the tunnels of time.

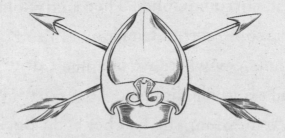

CHAPTER 2
ISIS GOES HOME

"Wheeeee!" Tom cried.

Thunk! Thunk! Thunk! The three travellers shot out of the time tunnels into hot, dry air and blinding sunlight. They landed on the dusty ground. Tom looked round and saw an enormous river, twisting like a dark green snake into the distance. Closer by, there was a grid of buildings with golden desert beyond.

Tom gazed up at scaffolding made from tree trunks. Men were scurrying up and down it, carrying stones. They seemed to be building some sort of temple.

"You know where we are, don't you?" Isis said excitedly, gripping Tom's arm. No longer a mummy, she had her body back again. Her kohl-lined eyes shone with glee.

"Not really," Tom said, looking down at their white linen tunics.

Cleo purred loudly then stretched out her legs and licked her stripy fur. Isis scooped the cat into her arms.

"We're home, Fluffpot!" she said. "I'd know that river anywhere. It's the Nile!"

"Ancient Egypt?" Tom said, staring at the builders. They had the same dark skin as Isis. Some were bald, but others wore ponytails.

"Cool! Where's your palace then?"

Isis shielded her eyes from the sun and peered round. "Good question. To be honest, I don't recognise any of these buildings. There's not a pyramid in sight."

Tom called over to a worker, who was lifting a basket full of mud on to his broad shoulders. "Excuse me," he said. "What city are we in?"

The worker frowned at him.

Tom wondered if the man hadn't understood him. So far, thanks to Anubis's magic, he and Isis had been able to speak to people in every time and place they had visited. Had the magic worn off?

"The capital, of course!" the man finally said, to Tom's relief.

"Memphis?" Isis asked, looking hopeful.

As he started to climb the scaffold, the

man laughed. "No, Amarna, silly girl." He looked down at Isis and shook his head. "Do you think we're still in the Old Kingdom, or something?"

Tom expected Isis to tell the worker off for being so rude to a princess, but instead she just looked puzzled.

"I don't understand," she said. "I was sure me and Fluffpot had come home."

"Let's go and look over there," Tom said, pointing to a high stone wall that had already been finished. Two men were chiselling away, covering the wall in hieroglyphics.

"Those men are scribes," Isis said. "This must be a temple of some sort."

When they reached the wall, Isis pointed excitedly at a figure carved into the stone.

"Look!" she said. "Here's a picture of my

31

father." She smiled as she traced the carved surface with her fingertips. "Everyone used to tell me I looked just like him."

Tom looked at the carving, but couldn't see much of a resemblance.

"We *are* in Egypt," Isis said, studying the wall. "But judging from how old this carving looks, it seems we've turned up long after I was alive."

As she spoke, there was the sound of splitting rock above them. Tom looked up and saw three men pushing the head off the biggest statue he had ever seen. It slowly rolled forward and then...

CRASH!

The whole statue came tumbling down.
Cleo darted out of its way. Tom grabbed Isis,
and they stumbled backwards as bits of stone
smashed all round them.

"Whoa!" Tom cried. "That thing nearly killed us!"

"This is too dangerous, even for someone as brave as me!" said Isis. "Let's find my amulet and get out of here."

"The ring," Tom said. "Ask your ring for help."

Isis looked down at her magical scarab ring, which had once belonged to the goddess Isis herself.

"Oh, goddess Isis," she began. "Please help us one last time. Tell us where we can find the final amulet!"

Silvery words drifted up out of the ring and hung in the air in the shape of a riddle.

Tom cleared his throat and read out loud:

"From the north, ill tides do flow,
As neighbours seek to breach the bank.

Into battle you must go,
If you want to find what's in the ankh.
This final quest has brought you home,
But the kingdom's threat is very real.
Seek the boy king! Crush his foe,
Beneath the chariot's mighty wheel."

"What does that mean?"
Tom said. "For a start,
what's an ankh?"

"It's an Ancient
Egyptian symbol that
means the key to life,"
Isis said, watching the
silvery words disappear.

Tom was wondering
whether the words 'ill tides do flow' and
'breach the bank' had anything to do
with the River Nile, when a gruff voice

shouted, "You two! Get over here and stop slacking!"

Swinging round, Tom spotted a short man with a bald head and an enormous pot belly that hung over his loincloth. In his hand was a large whip.

"Somebody's been eating more than his fair share of cake," Isis giggled.

With the pot-bellied foreman cracking his whip at their heels, Tom and Isis were forced to join a group of workers pulling a sledge across rolling logs. The sledge held a giant lump of stone.

Tom grabbed the rope.

"HEAVE!" the foreman yelled. His whip snapped on a worker's back. "HEAVE!"

The sledge hardly moved an inch, even with everyone pulling. Tom could feel the scratchy rope biting into his hands. To make matters worse, the sun blazed down on his head.

"This is not a job for a princess!" Isis gasped.

Crack! went the whip. "Get on with it, boy!" the foreman barked at her.

Isis's eyebrows bunched together. "Boy? I'm not a boy — I'm a princess. I'm going to teach that bully a lesson!" she hissed, throwing the rope to the ground.

"No, Isis! Don't—"

Tom reached out to stop her, and lost his grip on the rope.

"No!" he cried.

Too late! Tom stumbled and several huge, muscly builders piled on top of him and Isis, as the entire line gave way. From underneath the mountain of workers, Tom spied a very angry-looking foreman.

"You! Get over here!" he snarled at Tom, cracking his whip. "I'm going to give you the thrashing of your life!"

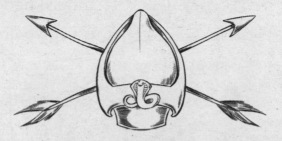

CHAPTER 3
THE BOY KING

Snap! The foreman's whip whizzed through the air and cracked on the sand, right by Tom's feet.

"I don't have time for weaklings!" the foreman shouted, grinning nastily.

Tom braced himself for the whip's sting. But suddenly a young man, dressed in a pleated loincloth, ran up to the foreman. He whispered urgently in his ear.

The foreman frowned at Tom and Isis.

"It's your lucky day – I don't have time to
give you a beating. Get over to the old temple
wall and help chisel off the picture of Aten!"
He pointed at a stone building in the distance.

Tom, Isis and Cleo ran off before he could change his mind.

The temple was full of workers hacking away at a picture of a large disc carved into a lump of pink granite.

"Yikes. That was close," Tom said. "Who's this Aten?"

Isis shrugged. "I don't know," she said.

One of the workers, who'd stopped chiselling to wipe his sweaty brow, looked at Isis and chuckled. He pointed to the disc.

"This is Aten, silly!" he said. "The Sun God, of course."

"Nonsense!" Isis scoffed. "Everyone knows the Sun God and creator of all things is Ra! Amun-Ra!"

"What? Where have you two been?" the man asked. "The whole reason we're getting rid of this carving is because the old pharaoh made everyone worship just one god, Aten. His son, the new pharaoh, has gone back to worshipping the old gods — so there's a lot of work for us changing all the temples back."

"Quite right," Isis said, frowning at the giant carved disc. "Whoever heard of having just one god? How ridiculous!"

Seeing a new foreman glaring at them, Tom and Isis each picked up a chisel and hammer and began chipping away at the rock. Even Cleo scratched at the carving with her claws.

After a while, Isis groaned. "This is the most boring thing I've ever done," she complained.

"More boring than being stuck in a statue for five thousand years?" Tom asked.

Isis rolled her eyes. Then she started to chisel her own marks into the granite. Tom watched a picture take shape beneath her tools.

"What's that?" he asked.

There was a stick figure with wings, standing next to a large circle. The stick figure had its hands on its hips.

"See that?" Isis said proudly. "That's the goddess Isis."

"What's that thing coming out of her mouth?" Tom asked.

"She's sticking out her tongue at Aten, obviously!"

"Obviously," said Tom, squinting at the little cartoon in the stone. He spied another stick figure with pointy ears, bending over. "Who's this meant to be?"

Isis started to giggle. "That's Anubis wiggling his bum at Aten."

Tom laughed.

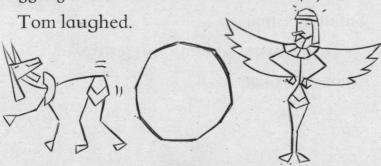

Suddenly, a loud tooting sound rang out through the temple. There was the scuffle of sandalled feet. Tom looked round and saw the foreman blowing a horn. *Toot! TOOOOOT!*

"Listen up, you lazy lot!" the foreman shouted out to the groups of builders and craftsmen. "King Tutankhamun is coming to inspect the temple, so you'd better be on your best behaviour!" He shook his whip. "Or you'll answer to *this*."

The foreman blew his horn in Isis's face, then strode to the other side of the temple courtyard.

Tom turned to Isis. "Did you hear who's coming?" he asked excitedly. "King Tuthankhamun!"

"Never heard of him," Isis grumbled, rubbing her ear.

Tom gasped. "I can't believe you haven't heard of King Tut. He's only the most famous Ancient Egyptian pharaoh ever!" Grinning, he told Isis all about Howard Carter's discovery of King Tutankhamun's tomb. "His tomb was stuffed full of treasure! Statues, gold, jewellery and even mummified servants..."

"I bet my tomb was full of lovely things too," Isis said, looking a little put out.

"Well, King Tut's tomb was special, because by the time it was discovered most pharaohs' tombs had been raided by thieves. And get this! He was really young when he became Pharaoh." Tom looked down at Isis's scarab ring, suddenly remembering the words of the riddle. "Hang on a minute," he said. "The riddle tells us to 'seek a boy king', doesn't it? It must be him!"

Isis started to jump up and down with excitement. "So King Tut will help us find the amulet!" she squealed.

Tom and Isis stared as the legendary boy king made his grand entrance to the temple. Except that, apart from more horn-tooting, it wasn't very grand at all.

"*That's* King Tut?" Tom said out of the corner of his mouth. "He's limping!"

Isis shielded her eyes from the blazing sun and squinted at the king. "My father was a *much* more impressive-looking pharaoh. This one looks like they tried to wash him in the Nile and he shrank!" She started to giggle.

As King Tutankhamun hobbled towards them, his skinny body looked as though it was about to crumple under the weight of his gold jewelled collar.

Two older men stood either side of him.

One was wearing a leather tunic covered
in metal scales, like armour. The other was
dressed like the king, in a linen kilt. Servants
waved cool air on them all, using giant,
feathered fans.

"King Tut looks bored listening to those old guys!" Tom said. He strained to hear what the men were saying.

"I tell you, Egypt is going to be invaded any day now," the man in the leather tunic said to the other man. "You're the royal vizier. After the pharaoh, you have the most important job in the entire kingdom. Tell His Royal Highness that we must take action!"

"General Horemheb, the Hittites would never dare invade Egypt," the vizier said, frowning.

"Who are the Hittites?" Tom whispered to Isis.

"They're the people who live north of Egypt," explained Isis. "They're our enemies, but they're no match for the Egyptians."

"How are we going to get close to the

48

king?" Tom said. "Maybe we should try to distract his minders…"

"I've got a better idea," Isis said. "Watch this!"

Isis unexpectedly darted out from the huddle of builders that had gathered to greet their king.

"Yoo-hoo, Your Royal Highness!" she shouted to King Tut, waving frantically. "I'm Princess Isis Amun-Ra from—"

General Horemheb whipped out his sword. He pointed the gleaming tip at Isis's throat.

"Nobody comes near the king!" he snarled. "Get back!"

Tom hurried over and pulled Isis away from the blade.

"What are you doing?" Isis hissed.

"Saving your skin!" Tom said. "Dying once is bad enough. Dying twice is plain silly."

49

Isis folded her arms. She glared at the general and then turned to Tom. "How else are we going to get near the king? We might not get another chance!"

Tom racked his brains for a plan. *We've got to attract his attention somehow*, he thought. "Hey! King Tut! We're your two biggest fans!" he cried out.

The boy king glanced over, still looking bored. Then his eyes came to rest on Isis's rude carving of the gods. King Tut froze, a strange look on his face.

Oh no! thought Tom. *We've offended the pharaoh!*

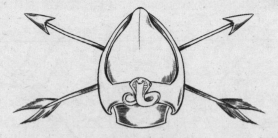

CHAPTER 4
FRIENDS IN HIGH PLACES

King Tut clutched at his stomach and bent over. He started to shake and made a terrible noise, like a braying donkey.

Tom gulped and bowed low. "Your R-royal Highness, I'm s-so sorry," he stuttered. "We didn't mean to upset you. We were just having a bit of fun. Please don't cry."

"Cry?" King Tut asked, straightening up. He grinned. "I'm not crying." He pointed

to Isis's carving. "I'm laughing! That's the
funniest thing I've ever seen!"

"Oh, phew," Tom said. "I'm Tom and this
here is—"

"Isis!" Isis said, pushing Tom aside. "Nice
to meet you." She gestured to Cleo, who was

playfully batting at a lizard. "This is my cat, Cleopatra."

"You two are funny!" said King Tut to Tom and Isis. "You've *got* to come to the palace and be my servants."

"Oh, thanks," Tom said. "We'd love to!"

General Horemheb put his right hand over his chest and bowed low. "Your Highness," he began, "you already have enough servants."

"Yes, definitely," Vizier Ay said, giving Tom a sour look. "We're on the brink of war with the Hittites. The last thing we need is to have people we don't know running about the palace." He looked at Tom's blonde hair and pale skin suspiciously. "What if he's a Hittite spy?" Ay asked.

"I'm not!" Tom snapped. "We're just travellers passing through."

"From where?" Ay said.

"Nowhere *you* will have heard of... but I'm *definitely* not a Hittite!"

Isis leaned in, her eyes twinkling mischievously. "Of course you'd say that even if you *were* a spy."

Tom crossed his arms and stared at her in disbelief. "Er, whose side are you on?" he asked.

Then King Tut stamped his foot so hard that everybody stopped arguing.

"*I'm* the pharaoh here!" he shouted, glaring at the vizier and the general. "It's *my* decision. They're coming to the palace and that's that!"

The king's outburst did the trick.

Ay shrugged his shoulders. "As you wish, Your Majesty."

Phew! thought Tom. They weren't just

getting close to the king – they were going to his palace! And, best of all, the famous pharaoh seemed pretty cool.

"Let's get out of here," Tut said merrily. Tom helped the boy king into a golden chariot that had two stallions harnessed to it. "I'll take you to the palace myself. This is going to be great!"

"Wait for me, Your Majesty!" General Horemheb shouted. "I'll drive you home!"

But King Tut just turned away as though he had not heard.

Isis stroked the carved sides of the chariot. "It's been a long time since we've travelled in one of these, hasn't it, Fluffpot?" she said, leaping aboard. Cleo meowed loudly and jumped into her arms.

It was a tight squeeze. With Isis and the

55

king hogging the front, Tom was balancing on the back. He almost fell out of the chariot when Tut flicked the reins and they started to roll away from the temple. Glancing behind him, Tom saw the grumpy-looking vizier and general piling into another chariot.

"Show us what it can do, then!" Isis said. "Come on! Let's go!"

King Tut nodded and grinned. "Get up, horses!" He flicked his whip and the stallions thundered away in a cloud of dust.

"Slow down, Your Highness!" the vizier called out. "Remember what the doctor said about your health!"

But Tut showed no signs of slowing. He shouted, "Yippee!" as Isis urged him to go faster and faster.

"Woo-hoo!" cried Tom, clinging on tightly. He felt like they were flying. In no time at all, they reached the palace.

Bringing the horses to a stop, King Tut climbed out of the chariot, clutching his sides with laughter.

"That was the best fun I've had in ages!" he said.

"Me too!" Tom said. He could see that the king's skin had gone from a sickly yellow to being flushed with healthy colour.

"Welcome to my home!" Tut said.

Tom gazed in awe at the stone walls that loomed above them, gleaming white in the strong Egyptian sun. He and Isis followed the king through a pair of golden gates, flanked on either side by giant pillars.

"Not bad!" Tom said, entering a grand stone hallway.

Suddenly, Ay's angry voice boomed out behind them. "Your Majesty! That was most unwise."

Tom turned round to see the grim face of the vizier. He looked furious! Next to him, General Horemheb was shaking his head.

"Very silly indeed! What if the chariot had crashed?" the general said.

King Tut waved away their concerns. "Nonsense! I'm a pharaoh, not a bird's egg. I don't break that easily. Now, I suppose you want to discuss the Hittite problem."

He waved goodbye to Tom and Isis and then limped after the vizier and the general, who were already marching across the hall. They stopped in front of a doorway, which was guarded by two tall soldiers holding spears. Tom watched as General Horemheb turned round and patted the king on his head.

"You don't need to trouble yourself with this boring meeting, Your Majesty. Leave it to me. Go and play with your new servants."

Tom cupped his hand round Isis's ear and whispered, "I think they're trying to get rid of him."

Isis nodded. "That bossy general thinks he's the real pharaoh."

But King Tut did as he was told and walked back over to Tom and Isis. "Come on," he said. "I'll show you round your new home."

Tom, Isis and Cleo were led through lofty stone halls decorated with huge paintings and hieroglyphics.

"Wow! This place is amazing," Tom said.

Isis merely sniffed. "It's OK, I suppose."

They wandered into a courtyard garden that was full of palm trees. Cleo ran straight

to the pond in the middle and swiped her
paw at a shadow in the water.

There was a shimmer and a splash as she
tossed a rainbow-coloured fish into the air.
Uh oh! thought Tom. *Now we'll be in trouble!*
But, unexpectedly, Tut started to chuckle as
Cleo plopped the fat fish at the king's feet.

"Is that a gift for me?" Tut asked. "Clever
girl!"

"Is she?" Tom asked, frowning.

"Yes!" said Isis, giving her cat a stroke.

Back inside the palace, the king led them
to the throne room. On a raised platform sat
a throne made from solid gold. Its surface
was studded with jewels. Carved into it was
a picture of King Tut throwing a spear at a
lion. The walls were decorated with more
paintings of him, winning battles or hunting
wild animals.

"This is so cool!" Tom said, impressed.

Isis waved her hand at the pictures. "Have you *really* done all these things?" she asked with a raised eyebrow.

King Tut shrugged. "No. It's just for show." He pointed to his bad foot. "I can't be a proper warrior king. Not with my limp."

"Nonsense!" Isis scoffed. "Of course you can. You shouldn't let General Horemheb and Vizier Ay boss you about."

Shaking his head, King Tut sighed. "Nobody really liked my father," he said. "He was unpopular because he forced everyone to start worshipping Aten. Now Egypt is a mess, and the Hittites are trying to grab power while we are weak." He slumped down into his golden throne. "General Horemheb says the country needs a strong leader, but that's not going to be me."

Tom leaped up. "You *can* be a great ruler, Your Highness. You've just got to believe in yourself."

With a grunt, the king stood up. "Maybe," he said, still sounding unconvinced. "Come on. Let me show you the rest of the palace."

Isis nudged Tom. She pointed to a symbol that looked like a cross with a loop at the top, which was painted on the wall. "Look, Tom! That's an *ankh*. Remember the riddle?"

"Now we just need to find one with an amulet inside it," Tom said, nodding.

As they wandered from room to room, Tom and Isis searched for ankhs. Now he knew what they looked like, Tom saw them everywhere.

As King Tut led them into a banqueting hall, Tom spotted a huge statue of Anubis at the far end. His heart pounded.

"Look!" Tom whispered. "Anubis is holding an ankh."

"There's a big purple stone in it," Isis whispered back. "That's the sixth amulet! I bet you a thousand scarabs!"

As Isis distracted Tut by asking him questions about the palace, Tom raced to the statue and tried to pry the purple gem out of the ankh.

Suddenly, the giant statue came to life. With a snarl, Anubis pushed Tom to the ground. His eyes glowing red with fury, the god plucked out the purple jewel and flung it at Tom, narrowly missing him.

"How DARE you damage my statue," he hissed furiously.

"I'm sorry," Tom said, gulping. "I thought it was the sixth amulet." But looking at the gem on the floor, he saw that it was a dull purple, rather than glowing with magic.

"You didn't think it would be *that* easy, did you?" sneered Anubis. "I warned you this would be your hardest challenge yet!"

Letting out a booming laugh, the god of the Underworld snapped his finger and gems rained down like hailstones, pelting Tom.

Tom hid his face in his hands until the shower of jewels finally stopped.

When he dared to look again, he saw that the statue of Anubis was just a statue once more, and the gems had vanished. But instead of feeling relieved, Tom felt more worried than ever.

There were ankhs and gems all over the palace. *How on earth are we ever going to find the amulet amongst so much other treasure?* He wondered. One thing was for sure — Anubis was right when he said it wasn't going to be easy.

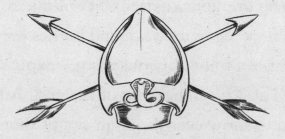

CHAPTER 5
PARTY POOPED

"Will you keep still?" Isis snapped at King Tut.

She was carefully painting kohl round the king's eyes.

Tut waved Isis away. "I'm so nervous," he told them. "Tom! Come over here and fan me."

Even though it was night-time, it was still hot. Tut walked over to the window and looked up at the full moon. Tom followed, waving a giant feathered fan.

"Why are you worried?" Tom asked. "You're going to a party, and parties are fun."

"This isn't just any old party," explained King Tut. "It's in honour of the god, Amun. I need to show everybody in Egypt that we're returning to the old ways. Hopefully, they'll all cheer up then, and I can drag the country out of the mess my dad got it into!"

"You'd better get ready then!" said Tom, pointing at the linen outfit laid out for the king.

Tut chuckled. "You too. You need some kohl round your eyes. A king's servants must always look their best." Tut clicked his fingers in Isis's direction. "Make him look presentable, Isis."

"Good idea! But less of the clicking, Tutty Boy!" Isis said, grinning. She rushed over to Tom, holding a fine brush loaded with the black goo.

"No way!" Tom cried, pushing her away. "Makeup is for girls!"

"No, it's not!" Isis said. "In Ancient Egypt we used it to protect our eyes from infection and the rays of the sun. You should know that, Professor Smartypants!" She smiled smugly at Tom. "Besides, I've had to disguise myself as a boy on our adventures – so it's only fair that you wear this kohl."

Although he hated the way the brush tickled, Tom groaned and let Isis paint round his eyes.

When Tut had finished dressing, Tom and Isis helped the king put on his jewellery. Tom lifted a heavy collar that had been hanging on a stand by the bed.

"Wow! This weighs a ton," Tom said.

"It's solid gold, studded with precious stones," Tut said. "It looks fancy, but wearing it makes my neck ache."

Tom spotted an ankh containing a gem that looked very much like one of Anubis's amulets.

"Look at that!" he whispered, nudging Isis and pointing at the ankh. "Do you think that could be the sixth amulet?"

Isis squinted at the bright stone, sighed and then shook her head sadly. "I don't think so."

Once again, Tom wondered if Anubis had set them an impossible task.

As he strode into the torch-lit banqueting hall behind King Tut, Tom's glum mood lifted. The hall was packed with richly dressed people. All the guests, even the men, were wearing makeup, jewels and headdresses.

"It's like a fancy dress party," Tom said to Isis.

"They look gorgeous, don't they?" Isis sighed, staring at all the ladies' dresses.

Balanced on top of everyone's head were wax cones. As they melted slowly, they filled the air with sweet-smelling incense. In a corner of the room, musicians were playing a harp, a flute, a lyre and a lute. Best of all, the tables were spread with a feast.

Cleo didn't wait to be invited. She sneaked

a fish from a platter and gobbled it down.

"What is all that?" Tom asked Isis, eyeing the strange dishes.

Isis rubbed her tummy. "Oh, *proper* food!" She grabbed a hunk of meat and sandwiched it in a flatbread. "There's all sorts of yummy things here. Gazelle, pelican..."

"I love nuts!" Tom said, grabbing a handful. Then he helped himself to some pelican. It tasted a little like roast chicken. "A bit chewy, but not bad at all." Next, Tom started to eat some bread. "Aargh! There's grit in this!"

"A bit of sand won't hurt you, silly!" Isis passed him a goblet of some strange-looking liquid. "Here," she said. "Wash it down with some beer."

Tom peered into the goblet and saw some odd, floating lumps. "Er... no thanks," he said. "It looks worse than pirate grog."

King Tut took his place on a throne at the far end of the hall. Isis and Tom were ordered to stand on either side of him while the guests came forward to greet their king.

"The fine lady Neferet," Vizier Ay announced, as the ugliest old woman Tom had ever seen shuffled up to Tut.

Her teeth were black stumps. She was so overloaded with jewels that she walked with a stoop. She eyed up Tut and snorted. "How's a little boy going to defend Egypt?" Shaking her head, she added, "And the meat in the buffet was too tough. I couldn't chew it!"

"Those teeth would find anything hard to chew," Tom whispered to Isis and Tut.

Tut erupted into a fit of giggles, which soon got rid of the old woman.

The next to approach was a tall man dripping in gold jewellery. He was even more finely dressed than King Tut.

"The chief of police, the great Mahu!" Vizier Ay announced.

"Your Majesty is so gracious and strong and handsome!" Mahu said with a fake smile. "But if *only* he could give me more gold, I could keep the kingdom much safer."

"Judging from the amount of gold he's wearing, you pay him plenty already," muttered Isis.

This time, Tut laughed right in Mahu's face and the chief of police walked away scowling.

Tom thought about the riddle saying a

74

'neighbour from the north'. Could one of the guests be the neighbour?

Tut clapped his hands. "Let's have some music, Isis," he said. "We need to liven up this party."

Isis grabbed a lyre from one of the musicians and started to strum its strings.

"As you already know, I'm very musical," she boasted to Tom, who rolled his eyes.

As Isis's quick fingers played a lively tune, the party guests began to dance. Even Cleo and the palace cats joined in. Tom tapped his toes from the side of the dance floor. It wasn't exactly his sort of music, but he had to admit that Isis was talented.

The fun didn't last for long. Suddenly, a messenger ran into the banquet hall.

"Egypt is under attack!" he cried. "The Hittites have crossed the sea and invaded."

Before King Tut could say a word, the guests panicked. Everyone stampeded towards the courtyard garden and one party guest slipped on a banana skin and fell into the pond. The buffet table was

knocked over and an ostrich egg the size
of Tom's head hurtled through the air
towards him. He ducked just in time. It
landed with a loud splat on the chief of
police's head.

"Shall we get you somewhere safe, Your Highness?" Tom asked, trying to help the king out of his throne.

King Tut shook his head. "It's all right, Tom. I'm staying put. Let all the guests go! Then I'll have some peace and quiet."

Shouting at each other, General Horemheb and Ay marched up to the king.

The general spoke first. "We must go to war!" he snapped.

"Nonsense!" said the vizier. "*I* think we should speak with the Hittite leader and sort this out. You must reason with him, King Tut!"

Tom nudged Isis. "So the Hittites are what the riddle was talking about! They're the northern neighbours, planning to conquer the banks of the Nile."

Isis nodded slowly. She turned to face King Tut.

"What do *you* think?" she asked him. "Are you just going to let those Hittites invade Egypt?"

Tut looked at the stern faces of the vizier and the general. Then, gripping the arm of the throne, he rose and stood as tall and straight as he could.

"No," he announced. "And what's more, *I'm* going to lead the army into battle!"

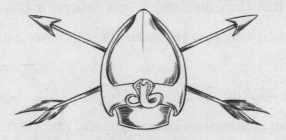

CHAPTER 6
KING OF THE JUNGLE

"You? Lead an army? What utter nonsense!"
General Horemheb scoffed. "You're far too
weak. You're an invalid, not a warrior!"

Tut looked at the floor and his shoulders
slumped.

Tom clenched his fists. "That's typical,"
he muttered. "Grown-ups always think they
know best, even when they don't."
He stepped forward, hands on his hips.

"Tut is a *very* fierce warrior, actually,"

Tom told the general. "And he can prove it!"

"I can?" Tut asked doubtfully.

Isis clapped him on the back. "Of course you can!" she said.

General Horemheb folded his thick, hairy arms over his leather tunic. "Very well," he said. His eyes narrowed. "If you can go hunting and bring back something big – and I mean *really big*, like a lion – then we'll know you've got the skill and courage needed to lead an army in battle."

Then the general started to snigger. It was obvious to Tom that he didn't think Tut could complete the task *or* lead an army.

Tut gulped. "Right. Then I will!" he said
in a shaky voice.

You can, Tut! Tom thought. *You really can!*
He knew that the king didn't believe he
could succeed, but luckily Tut had Tom
and Isis to help him. It wasn't going to
be easy to turn the boy king into a fierce
warrior – but no challenge had ever stopped
them before!

"Cheer up, boys! I've seen camels look
happier than you two," Isis said to Tom and
Tut as they climbed into the king's chariot.
"Tutty Boy here is going to be a
big success!"

Tom looked at Tut, who was getting
tangled up in his bow and quiver full of
arrows.

"Do you really think so?" King Tut asked.

"Of course," Isis said, winking. "You've got a brilliant teacher – me!"

Tut shook the reins and the horses pulled the chariot slowly out of the palace grounds. Before long, they picked up speed. Tom closed his eyes and enjoyed the wind whipping through his hair as they raced towards the dry, sandy desert.

"I'm going to be terrible on the battlefield," Tut said, sighing. "How can I fight with my bad leg? Maybe General Horemheb was right – I'm not strong enough to be a warrior king."

"Strength isn't the only thing a warrior needs," said Tom. "Brains and bravery are just as important." He thought back to all the opponents he and Isis had fought — powerful pirates, vicious Vikings, and great big gladiators. Even though they had been

83

much smaller, Tom and Isis had managed to defeat them all.

"Listen, as long as you can use your bow and arrow, you'll be fine," Isis said. "Plus, you've got a fantastic chariot."

As they flew over the rocky ground, Tom had to agree – riding in a chariot was even more fun than he could ever have imagined. He'd happily trade his bike for one any day!

"You don't need to be the fastest sprinter in Egypt to be a great pharaoh," Isis continued. "But you do need to be a good hunter if you're going to win the respect of your people. So I'm going to teach you how."

Tut raised an eyebrow at her. "You seem to know an awful lot about being a pharaoh."

Isis giggled. "Natural wisdom," she said.

Before long, the dry plains ended and the

path became lined with long grass and trees. Tut reined in the horses and the chariot came to a halt near a large tree.

"Pass me your bow and arrow," Isis told the king. "I'll teach you how to use them."

Isis walked fifty paces away from the tree. "Target practice," she explained. "Tut, you'll start here and then move further away as you get better."

She nocked an arrow and fired it straight into the trunk of the tree. It hit the target with a satisfying *thwack*. Isis grinned.

"You're such a good shot!" Tut said, clearly impressed.

"My father taught me," Isis explained. "He was an expert hunter. And soon you will be too. Thanks to me, obviously."

Isis passed the bow and arrow to Tut, who fumbled with it but eventually fired a shot.

"It's nowhere near!" Tut moaned, as the arrow sped past the tree trunk.

"Never mind," Isis said. "Just keep practising. And always get your next arrow ready as soon as you've fired one." She turned

to Tom. "You'll have to collect the spent arrows or he's going to run out."

Tom didn't like being bossed about by Isis, but he knew they had to work as a team if they were going to help King Tut and get the amulet.

One shot after another missed the tree trunk completely.

Tut flung his bow on the ground. "Oh, it's hopeless. I just can't do it!"

"Again!" Isis demanded, handing the bow back to him. "And this time, aim more to the left. You've got to allow for the breeze."

After what felt like hours, Tut's arrows finally started hitting the target.

"Right, now you've got to try to shoot something while you're on the move," Isis said.

Tom, Isis, Tut and Cleo piled back into the chariot. Tom held the reins.

"Yeeee-ha!" he cried as the chariot thundered off over the plains.

"See that clump of trees in the distance?" Isis shouted. "Try to hit them as we go past!"

As the chariot sped over the bumpy ground, it startled a herd of grazing gazelles. On long, nimble legs, the gazelles took off across the plain, kicking up a cloud of dust.

As they approached the trees, Isis instructed Tut, who took aim.

Tom skilfully steered the horses through the trees. They swerved round one tree trunk so fast that the chariot tilted on to its side.

"Now!" Isis cried, and Tut fired off an arrow.

One, two, three arrows pinged their way towards the trees... but not a single one found its mark. The arrows landed in the sandy soil.

Tom brought the horses to a halt. Panting and red-faced, King Tut slumped down to the floor of the chariot.

"I didn't hit *anything*," he said, sighing.

"You will next time," Isis said, passing him the water bottle.

Suddenly, Cleo yowled and hissed. Her fur stood on end and she cowered at the bottom of the chariot.

"What is it, Fluffpot?" Isis asked.

They all peered into the long grass. Then Tom saw the problem. It was golden, with the biggest, shaggiest mane he had ever seen. And it was stalking towards them!

"A lion!" he whispered.

Tom looked at Tut, who was clinging on to his bow and arrow, frozen with fear.

"Tut, you need to do something!" Tom said.

"I can't," Tut said, trembling. "I can't even hit a tree!"

Tom knew he had to take charge.

"You can," he said, in a voice that was a

lot calmer than he felt. "Get the lion in your sights and fire."

The lion let out a low growl and flicked its tail. It took a step closer to the chariot, never taking its yellow eyes off them.

Tut took aim with his bow and arrow. His arm shook a little.

"When you're ready, take the shot," Tom said.

Tut let off his arrow. Tom bit his lip as he watched the arrowhead whizz through the air. It was a good shot, but at the last second the lion tossed his head and the arrow just grazed his ear.

The wounded lion reared up on its hind legs, towering above them.

RRRRROOOOOOOOOAAARRR!

The sound was deafening. The lion's jaw opened wide, flashing teeth as sharp as

daggers. The ground beneath them shook as
the lion charged at the chariot.

Tom gulped – he was out of ideas...

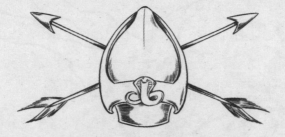

CHAPTER 7
A NILE CRUISE

The lion let out another deafening roar. It was so close, Tom could see the fury in its eyes.

In a flash, Isis grabbed the bow and arrow from Tut and took aim at the lion.

Whizz... thwack! The arrow flew through the air and struck the lion right between its eyes. The snarling creature slumped to the ground.

Tom bent over and clasped his knees

with relief. "That was close!" he said.

"I don't believe it!" said Tut, staring at the dead animal. "You saved us, Isis! You're a hero!"

Tom looked down at the lion and felt sad that his friend had had to kill such a magnificent beast. But he knew that she had saved their lives.

Isis didn't seem troubled by the lion's death, but Tom understood that it was because in Ancient Egyptian times, hunting wasn't just for sport, it was for survival. Isis polished her nails on her linen dress. "Ready to head back?" she said, smiling.

Tut suddenly looked worried.

"But *I'm* supposed to have killed the lion," he said. "If I return to the palace empty-handed, the general will—"

"Nobody needs to know it wasn't *you*,"

Tom said. "Besides, you did hit its ear."

With the lion's body strapped to the back of the chariot, the hunters began the journey home. As they rode through the dusty streets that led to the palace, people stopped and stared.

"Look!" one woman cried. "King Tut has killed an enormous lion!"

"The gods favour the king!" a man yelled.

Everybody started to join in. "King Tut is blessed by the gods," they shouted. "Our leader will save us from the Hittites."

The Egyptian people clapped and cheered them all the way to the palace. "You're a star," Tom told Tut. "They love you."

Tut smiled half-heartedly. "They all think I'm a warrior king," he said. "They wouldn't be cheering so loudly if they knew the truth."

"It doesn't matter who killed the lion," Isis said. "The main thing is you're ready to lead your army into battle now. The Egyptian people wanted a strong leader, and now they've got one!"

Tut looked at the lion and bit his lip. "I don't know if I'm ready to fight a war," he said. "At least, not without you two – I owe you both my life."

Casting his mind back to the riddle, Tom suddenly remembered the line about crushing the boy king's foe beneath the chariot's wheel. Going into battle would be dangerous; more dangerous than any challenge they had faced so far. But if they wanted to break Anubis's curse, there was no other way. *If we're going to find the amulet, we've got to stick close to Tut*, he thought. After everything he and Isis had been through together, there was no way they would give up now.

"We'll go into battle with you," Tom said, as he helped the king out of the chariot. "Won't we, Isis?"

Isis nodded. "Of course. We'll be by your side all the way."

"Oh, all right then," General Horemheb said to Tut. He wore a sour expression on his face. "You can lead the troops into battle." He turned to Tom and Isis and pointed. "But I don't want these two going with you."

"Hey! What's wrong with us?" Isis demanded.

The general thumped the table, which made the vizier's drinking goblet wobble.

"Because having one child in battle is bad enough," he said. "But *three*? That's utterly foolish! You would be nothing but trouble."

Vizier Ay cleared his throat and nodded.

He fixed his beady black eyes on Tom. "Besides, I still don't trust this one," he said.

"What are you talking about?" Tom asked, feeling his anger rising.

Vizier Ay leaned in and scowled. "It's funny how the Hittites invaded just as you appeared! Suspicious, don't you think? You will not be at the battle."

Tom and Isis exchanged a worried look as they saw their chance of finding the amulet slipping away.

"We *promised* to stand by King Tut!" Isis said.

"No!" both the general and vizier said.

King Tut stood up quickly, knocking his chair backwards. "The last time I checked, I was the only pharaoh in this room," he said in a sure, strong voice that surprised Tom. "I need my servants' help. So they're coming with me and that's final!"

"On to the barge! Quick march!" General
Horemheb yelled at the troop of soldiers.

Tom was surprised to see that the soldiers
were not wearing uniforms or armour – just
plain white loincloths. They were carrying
everything the Egyptian army would need for
the battle. Tom watched with excitement as
they rolled chariots below deck and carried
shields, spears, bows and arrows aboard.

"Follow me," Tut told Tom and Isis. He started to walk up the gangplank.

Cleo, who was terrified of water, clung to the wooden gangplank with her claws.

"Don't worry, Fluffpot," Isis said, scooping up her cat and tickling her under the chin. "It's the last time I'll make you get on a boat — I promise! With a bit of luck, we'll be in the Afterlife soon."

Tut was wearing a tall blue crown that doubled as a helmet. There was a golden cobra attached to the forehead. *That is so cool!* Tom thought. *Dad would love to get his hands on one of those for the museum!*

The loaded barge set sail up the Nile.

"We're going north," Tut explained. "That's where the border with the Hittite territory is."

As Tom held a sunshade over the king, he gazed at the passing scenery. Papyrus plants and palm trees lined the riverbank. Beyond the bank grew green fields of fruit and vegetables. Farmers tilled the land with water buffaloes harnessed to ploughs. They sailed past majestic tombs and temples built close to the water. Cheetahs, gazelles and hippos came down to the river to drink. As the barge sailed further north, sandy mountains rose up in the distance.

"Where are we stopping?" Isis asked Tut, interrupting Tom's daydreams.

The king shrugged. "I'm not sure. Nobody really knows where the enemy's army is gathered. General Horemheb just wants to join forces with the whole Egyptian army and march north until we meet the Hittite troops."

Tom frowned. He checked that Horemheb wasn't eavesdropping and lowered his voice. "Listen, Tut. Lumping your entire army into a single unit sounds madness. What if the Hittites have separated and you're ambushed from two different directions?"

Tut's eyes narrowed. "Then we'll be surrounded and I could lose all my men at once."

"Exactly," Tom said. "If I were you, I'd split your army into two divisions. It's less risky."

Tut nodded. He called General Horemheb and Vizier Ay over and told them his plan. They protested loudly.

"Your Majesty, I can't—" the general began.

Tut clapped his hands, silencing the two men. "Having two divisions is a *much* more sensible idea. So that's what we're going to do. I will lead the Isis squadron."

Isis sighed with satisfaction at the mention of her name.

"He's named it after the goddess, not you!" said Tom.

"And you, general, will lead the Anubis squadron," Tut finished.

"As you wish, Your Highness," the general said, bowing low.

"It's so beautiful in Egypt," Tom said, when Tut had gone off with the general to study maps of the north. "The scenery, the animals, the buildings... all of it."

Isis smiled. "Egypt is the best place on earth. That's why we need to protect it and kick the Hittites out." Then her smile disappeared. "But being here makes me miss my family terribly. I want to get into the Afterlife more than ever so I can see them again." She looked grim-faced. "We've *got* to find the last amulet, Tom."

Tom put his hand on her shoulder. "We will, Isis. I promise."

Cold laughter suddenly rippled through the air. "Don't be so sure, you cheeky children!" cackled Anubis.

An almighty wind blew up. The calm waters of the Nile started to churn as if a storm was coming, even though the skies were still clear.

The barge lurched to the side, sending anything that wasn't fastened down sliding along the deck.

"We're going to capsize!" Isis yelled.

Before Tom knew what was happening, Ay stumbled towards them.

"You, boy!" the vizier bellowed. "I knew you weren't to be trusted! You have upset the gods!" He grabbed Tom by the collar and dragged him to the edge of the barge.

Tom stared into the murky water. "What are you doing?" he cried.

"I'm tossing you into the Nile to appease the gods!" Ay declared. "Hope you Hittites know how to swim!"

"I'm not a Hittite!" Tom protested, clinging to the side of the barge.

But it was no use – Ay flung Tom overboard and into the Nile with a *splash*!

As Tom ducked below the surface, he heard Anubis's cruel laughter ringing in his ears.

"Enjoy your swim!" the god's voice boomed.

At least the river's warm, Tom thought, treading water.

"Grab this!" Isis shouted, throwing a rope over the side of the barge. But as Anubis laughed again, the end of the rope got tangled in a clump of reeds.

Tom looked round for something else to grab, and spotted a log floating nearby. He started swimming towards it. *Nearly there*, he thought. But as he drew closer, he realised the log had eyes. Then he noticed its teeth — big, sharp teeth.

"A crocodile!" Tom yelled.

He racked his brains to remember what he had seen on nature programmes on television about crocodiles.

His mind was completely blank.

The huge reptile drifted through the water towards him. Its eyes blinked lazily and its jaws opened wide...

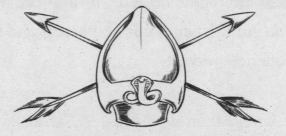

CHAPTER 8
SURPRISE ATTACK

"Help!" Tom screamed, desperately trying to swim away.

Just as the crocodile was about to snap its deadly jaws shut round him, there was a whizzing sound and – *thwack!* – an arrow lodged itself right in the crocodile's head. The scaly beast sank to the bottom of the Nile with only a few bubbles on the surface of the water to show that it had ever been there.

Tom looked up and saw the king standing

on deck, holding his bow. He was beaming.

"You did it!" Tom shouted. "Amazing!"

"I couldn't very well let a crocodile eat my friend," Tut said, standing tall and looking more kingly than he had ever seemed before. "What can I say? I've had great teachers," he added, grinning at Isis.

"Quick, Tom!" Isis yelled. She held out an oar. "Grab this!"

Swimming back to the boat as quickly as he could, Tom reached for the oar. But the vizier appeared at Tut's side.

"Leave the Hittite spy for the crocodiles, Your Majesty," he said.

Ay tried to snatch the oar out of Isis's hands, but Tut stood firm.

"Step back!" the king commanded. "My friend isn't a Hittite, and I say he gets back on the boat."

The vizier stormed off to the other end of the barge as Isis and Tut pulled a sopping-wet Tom back on board.

"I know you like the wildlife here, but no more throwing yourself at the crocodiles, OK?" Isis said, offering him a cloth to dry off with.

"Don't worry," Tom said, looking into the murky water. "I'm not planning on going for another dip in the Nile."

As the water became calm again, the barge sailed smoothly on towards the north. Tom dried off quickly in the hot sun.

At last the barge was moored and the equipment and horses were carried on to dry land. The troops gathered on the riverbank, looking serious.

Cleo, however, meowed happily. She wriggled out of Isis's arms and padded a safe distance from the water.

"I think somebody prefers fighting to sailing," Isis told Tom, as they both took their places at Tut's side.

"Men! Split into two divisions!" Tut ordered his troops.

As the soldiers gathered their weapons, Tom, Isis and Tut armed themselves with shields. The shape of the shields reminded Tom of tombstones from ghost stories. They each took a bow and a quiver of arrows.

General Horemheb led his men off to the east. Tom, Isis and Tut climbed into Tut's gleaming chariot, and led the second squadron in a different direction.

The sun bounced off the cracked desert flats.

"So we're heading north?" Tom asked Tut, shielding his eyes against the glare.

"That's right," Tut said. "Towards the coast. I think we'll be travelling a good while before we see the enemy. The Hittites can't have got very far down into Egypt yet."

But only minutes later, there was a cry from a scout who was riding in a chariot ahead.

"The Hittites are coming!"

Sure enough, a dark line of chariots was carving its way quickly through the sand towards them. The line started to curve inwards as the Hittites closed in on Tut and his troops.

Willing his thumping heart to calm down, Tom studied the enemy as they came closer. Their metal helmets glinted in the sunlight. Tom could see that most of the Hittite men were carrying sharp spears and wore metal armour over long tunics. Even their horses were wearing armour!

"There are loads of them, and their chariots are massive compared to ours,!" Tom cried. "*And* we're not wearing any armour!"

King Tut nocked an arrow and raised his bow. "Who cares if we're outnumbered?" he said. "We're the greatest nation in the world.

CHAAAAARGE!" he yelled to his men.

The Hittite chariots thundered towards them, their arrows flying through the air.

"Shields up!" Tut called.

The arrows bounced off the Egyptians' shields. Tut's men returned fire.

Thwack! Thunk! The king fired off arrow after arrow, helping to keep the Hittites at a distance. But then a wall of heavy enemy chariots and armoured horses charged into the Egyptian soldiers.

Tom knew they were in real danger. He needed to get his friends to safety. Grabbing the reins, he quickly swung the royal chariot out of harm's way.

"Retreat! Retreat!" Tut shouted to his men.

As they fled away from the Hittites, Tom and Isis heard the bearded Hittite commander bellow after Tut, "We're going to control this land all the way to Thebes, little boy! That's right – limp home now!"

Tut led the battered soldiers back towards the river, where they sheltered behind some boulders.

"Should I just surrender?" Tut asked Isis and Tom.

Isis's eyes flashed. "Never!" she said. "It's your job to defend your country. Come on, Tut! Egypt needs you."

Tom scratched his head and tried to remember everything he had ever read about Ancient Egyptian, Greek and Roman battle tactics. An idea suddenly popped into his head.

"I've got it!" he said. "Your chariots are light and fast, right? And the Hittites chariots are big and clumsy."

"So?" said Tut.

"So, where are the Hittites camped?"

"My scouts told me they're at the base of a steep hill not far from here." Tut put his helmet on the ground and rubbed his temples.

Tom clicked his fingers. "Exactly! If we attacked them from above and shot our arrows *down* the hill, there's no way their horses could pull those heavy chariots up the hill quickly enough to fight back in time."

"You should listen to Tom!" Isis said. "I call him Professor Smartypants for a good reason – he's the smartest person I've ever met!"

"Really?" asked Tom, blushing.

"Really." Isis nodded. But then she winked and added, "But don't let it go to your head!"

Using an arrow, Tom started to scratch a little map in the sand.

"If the Isis division attacks here and then the Anubis division attacks from the other side—"

"The Hittites have their escape route

cut off," Tut finished Tom's sentence.
He beamed and put his helmet back on.
"Brilliant! This plan is so cunning. We need
to get word to General Horemheb – quickly!
And when his division has reached the top of
the hill, have him sound his horn three times
so my division will know to attack."

Tom was breathless with excitement as he,
Isis and Cleo rode a chariot over the desert
to where the Anubis division of soldiers was
gathered.

"I can't believe we're caught in the middle
of a historical battle between the Egyptians
and the Hittites!" Tom said excitedly. "Even
though we *still* haven't found the amulet."

Isis flicked the reins to make the horses
go faster. "We can worry about the amulet
later. Right now, we need to concentrate on

saving Egypt."

Cleo made a meowing noise and rubbed up against Isis loyally.

When the chariot rolled up to General Horemheb, Tom and Isis stumbled out.

"You need to come quickly!" Tom said, panting.

They told him all about the Hittites' deadly ambush.

"This is your fault!" General Horemheb barked, pointing at Tom. "I told the king we shouldn't have split up."

"But don't you see?" Tom began. "The Hittites think—"

"I don't want to hear another word from you, boy," Horemheb bellowed in Tom's face.

Isis stamped her foot. "Listen to Tom, you stubborn old goat! His plan is far cleverer

121

than anything you and that wrinkly old vizier could think up!" she shouted.

The general raised his whip at Isis but then seemed to think better of it. He pointed the handle at Tom. "What is this plan of yours, then, boy?" he asked.

"Well, the Hittites think the entire Egyptian army has been defeated now, don't they? They have no idea there's another division, waiting nearby. What we have now is the element of surprise!"

The general frowned. "What do you mean?"

Tom explained about attacking from the top of the hill.

"What do you say, General?" Isis asked. "Isn't it a good plan?"

"No!" General Horemheb barked. "It's not a good plan."

Tom's heart sank. King Tut had trusted them with an important mission, but they'd failed.

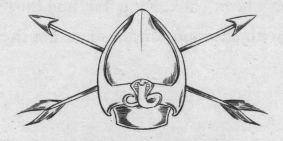

CHAPTER 9
THE KEY OF LIFE

General Horemheb clapped Tom on the shoulder. "It's not a good plan, boy. It's a *brilliant* plan!" he said. "We'll crush them!"

Tom stared at him in wonder. "You mean it?" he asked.

The general nodded just once. He turned his back on Tom and Isis and bellowed at his troops, "Prepare to attack, men!"

The Anubis division marched across the stony desert, sounding like thunder clouds crashing together. *Crunch, crunch, crunch* went their sandalled feet behind Tom and Isis's chariot.

"If you don't mind driving," Isis said, "I'll shoot." She twanged the string on her bow. "This is my homeland and I'm going to do everything I can to protect it."

Tom drove his horses up the hill that loomed over the Hittite camp. His heart was thudding like a drum. At the top, he pulled up the horses. The Anubis division ground to a halt behind him.

"Look!" he whispered to Isis. "See the black line and cloud of dust over there?"

Isis squinted into the distance. "Yes. It must be the Isis division," she said.

"We're ready," Tom said. He looked over his shoulder and nodded to the general.

The general picked up a horn and signalled

to Tut's division with three loud notes.

"Attack!" the general cried.

The Anubis division started to roll down the hill in a fierce avalanche of horses, chariot wheels and feet. Below them, the Hittite soldiers were panicking, as the Egyptian soldiers rained arrows down on them.

"Get up that hill!" Tom heard the Hittite leader shout.

But, as Tom had predicted, the Hittite chariots were clunky. Their horses reared and whinnied, unable to drag their heavy loads upwards. As the Isis division closed in from the opposition direction, the Hittites were trapped. They had no choice but to fight back.

"Archers, at the ready!" the Hittite leader yelled.

Tom looked up at the sky as it grew dark
with Hittite arrows.

"Take cover!" he called out to Isis.

Ping! Clank! Thwack! The arrows thudded
into the wooden sides of the chariot, or
bounced off the Egyptian shields.

Isis fired several arrows, but as the Hittites
launched another attack, Tom was forced to
swing the chariot round and head back up
the hill.

From the safety of the top, he gazed down into the mayhem of the battle below. He suddenly noticed a tall blue crown.

"Hey! Isn't that Tut?" he asked.

Just then, a Hittite spear flew straight towards the king. It punched into his armour with such force that Tut was thrown from his chariot.

"We've got to rescue him!" Tom cried in horror.

King Tut tried to stand up but fell down again. He was using his shield to protect himself from the trampling hooves and soldiers' feet that hammered the ground on all sides.

"Oh no!" Isis wailed. "He's badly injured. We need to get to him quickly, Tom, before he's crushed!"

Would they reach him in time?

"Yah!" Tom bellowed at his horses. He cracked the whip and steered the chariot down the hill at full speed, as Hittite arrows whizzed by.

Crashing through the Hittite ranks with gritted teeth, Tom and Isis finally reached Tut. Isis held out her hand to the boy king, just as an enormous Hittite soldier sprinted towards them with his sword drawn.

"Climb in!" Isis shrieked.

The soldier swiped at Tut, but Isis pulled the pharaoh out of harm's way and on to the chariot floor just in time.

"Take that!" Tom cried, slashing at the Hittite with his own sword in a deafening clang of metal.

Isis let sail arrow after arrow, which pinged off the soldier's armour.

Together, Tom and Isis fought tirelessly until, at last, the giant Hittite retreated.

"Come on!" Tom said. "Let's get Tut out of here!"

King Tut's army pounded the Hittites with wave after wave of chariot attacks, coming from all directions, thanks to Tom's plan.

After hours of fighting under the blazing sun, the Egyptians started to push the exhausted Hittites back towards the Red Sea.

"Retreat!" the Hittite leader finally shouted to his army.

"Yes, go on!" Isis yelled. "And don't come back! Egypt is *our* land, and it's not up for grabs."

With that, the Hittites turned their chariots and fled north.

Tut grinned at Tom and Isis. "I don't believe it!" he cried. "We've done it. We won!"

The entire Egyptian army cheered and tossed their helmets into the air. General Horemheb and Vizier Ay rode up to King Tut. They dismounted and bowed low.

"You did it, Your Royal Highness," the general said. He held his hand over his heart.

"I thought you were just a boy, but you are, in fact..." He started to cough, as though he was choking on the words, "...a great leader."

"Thanks be to the gods, for this incredible victory!" the vizier said, his eyes watering.

When the army had prayed to the gods, King Tut pulled Tom and Isis to one side.

"You know, my friends," he began. "I really couldn't have defeated the Hittites without you two. You helped me to believe in myself! And you saved my life again."

Isis blushed modestly. Tom bowed and grinned.

"Oh, it was nothing," Tom said. "You're our friend. You would have done the same for us."

Tut started to finger a thick golden chain

that hung round his neck. "But your battle plans, Tom, were the work of a genius. And, Isis, you took a helpless boy and turned him into a warrior king."

Isis started to chuckle. "Well, if you want to bring out the best in someone, you have to lead by example, don't you?" But turning serious, she added, "You already had what it takes to be a great leader."

Cleo, who had been curled up on the floor of the chariot, suddenly jumped up into Isis's arms. She nuzzled her mistress's cheek with her long whiskers and then offered Tut her paw.

"See, Fluffpot knows a true king when she sees one!" Isis said.

Tut beamed. Then he rummaged under his tunic's collar and pulled out something shiny that hung at the end of his gold chain. It was a large ankh. And in the centre of it was a giant purple amulet, which glittered in the afternoon sun.

Tom gasped – they'd been close to the sixth amulet all this time.

"I wore this ankh to protect me in battle," Tut said, picking the amulet out of its setting with careful fingers. "I want you to have this jewel. It's my way of saying thank you."

"It's beautiful," Isis said in wonder as she took the precious stone. She looked up at Tut. "Thank you. You really don't know how much this means to me."

"We have to go now," Tom said. "But we'll never forget you, King Tut. You'll always be remembered as one of Egypt's most famous pharaohs. Believe me."

Tut smiled. "Do you know? I do believe you, Tom."

135

As Tom, Isis and Cleo joined hands and paws, the amulet in Isis's palm glowed brightly. A gust of wind started to whip round their legs, sucking them up into the tunnels of time.

"Goodbye, King Tut!" Tom shouted over the wind to a waving, confused-looking Tut.

"See you in the Afterlife, Tutty Boy!" Isis called out.

The desert and the Egyptian army started to fade from view, as Tom, Isis and Cleo were whisked away through space and time.

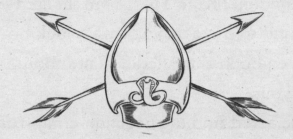

CHAPTER 10
FOND FAREWELL

Tom, Isis and Cleo shot through time into the bowling alley and found themselves back at Tom's party. They landed gently. Nobody gave them so much as a sideways glance. It was as if they had never been away.

"Would you like some more lemonade?" Tom's mum asked him.

Tom nodded and held out his glass. As Mum poured, Isis and Cleo — who were both back in their mummies' wrappings —

sat down on the end of the bench. Isis was staring in silence at the amulet in her hand.

"Pizza!" Dad shouted. "Come and get it!"

A waitress appeared, carrying a large silver tray full of delicious pizzas.

"Bowling and pizza is good," Isis said, "but it doesn't quite match up to King Tut's party, does it?"

"Not really," Tom said, taking a bite out of his pizza. "But I still like it." He took a hearty swig of his lemonade. "And this stuff tastes much better than that lumpy Egyptian beer!"

Isis sighed deeply. She pushed Cleo off her lap. She didn't even try to steal a slice of Tom's pizza.

"What's wrong with you?" Tom asked. "You should be happy."

Isis's fingers were tightly closed round the

amulet. "What if Anubis doesn't come?" she asked. "What if the whole thing was just a game to punish me for being cheeky?"

Tom could hear a nervous wobble in her voice. This wasn't like the confident, brave princess he knew.

"Hey! Come on," he said. "It will all be fine. You'll see." He searched his brain for comforting words. "If you've got the proper payment, even the god of the Underworld can't keep you out of the Afterlife, can he?"

Isis nodded and sat up straighter. "You're right," she said. Cleo leapt back on to her lap. "Even Anubis has to stick to the rules."

As she spoke, the red and blue neon lights in the bowling alley started to flash. Then there was a deafening *crash!* Every single bowling pin in the building toppled over.

"Yessssss!" Dad cried, completely unaware that an Ancient Egyptian god had just arrived at the party. "Strike!" He did a little victory dance.

Tom saw the towering figure of Anubis appear at the end of the bowling lane.

The jackal-headed god of the Underworld strode towards Tom and Isis, unseen by the other party guests. Anubis stepped nimbly over a fluorescent yellow ball that Tom's friend James had just bowled.

"Here you are," Isis said, meekly holding out the sixth amulet.

Anubis snatched it from her and held it up to the neon light. "Wouldn't it have been easier to give me all the amulets in the first place?" he demanded. His bushy eyebrows bunched together over his glowing red eyes. The nostrils in his doggy snout flared.

"Maybe," Isis said, nodding her head. "But it wouldn't have been as interesting."

"What's that?" Anubis barked. His pointy ears twitched. "Do my ears deceive me?"

Isis shrugged. "It might have been easier, but then I wouldn't have met Tom." She put her arm round Tom's shoulder. "He's the best friend a princess could ever want."

Tom grinned and looked at his feet.

"We had the most amazing adventures with him, didn't we, Fluffpot?" Isis continued.

Cleo rubbed her head against Tom's legs and meowed in agreement.

"We sure did," Tom said, suddenly feeling a bit lost for words.

Anubis folded his arms and licked his muzzle. "You have proven your bravery, little Isis Amun-Ra," he said. "And so has your friend. I suppose that means you have finally earned your place in the Afterlife!" The great god clapped his hands. "Isis and Cleo, prepare yourselves for a journey!" he bellowed. "It is time to leave the earthly world behind."

Isis started towards Anubis and then looked back at Tom.

"Wait a minute!" she said. She slipped off the magic scarab ring that had belonged to the goddess Isis herself. "Something to remember me by," she said, holding out the ring to Tom.

"But, Isis!" Tom gasped. "I couldn't possibly—"

"Keep it!" Isis said. "So you'll never forget me."

Tom clasped Isis into a hug. "I'd never do that," he said. "You're unforgettable."

Cleo meowed loudly.

"And so are you," he added, tickling the cat's bandaged ears. "I hope you enjoy the Afterlife."

A warm, gentle wind started to blow. Isis waved to Tom.

"Goodbye, Tom!" she called.

Gradually, Isis's bandaged arm turned into a living girl's arm. Tom watched in wonder, as Isis transformed back into a princess again. Then Cleo's bandages disappeared and she became a tabby cat once more, with tiger-like stripes and a fluffy tail.

The two glowed brightly and Isis gave him a dazzling smile. Tom swallowed hard as, led by Anubis, his friends disappeared into the Afterlife.

Tom stared at the space where his friends had been standing only a moment before.

"She's gone," he whispered to himself. "She's really gone. I don't believe it. All these weeks I've wanted to get rid of her, and now..."

In the pit of his belly, Tom had a strange, empty feeling. He frowned. Then he realised what it was.

I miss her, he thought. *And I'm going to miss our time-travelling adventures!*

Together they'd battled Roman gladiators, met the legendary King Arthur, shared a longship with Vikings, helped the Greek army break into Troy, sailed the high seas with the pirate Blackbeard, and fought the Hittites alongside King Tutankhamun.

Tom looked down at the scarab ring Isis had given him. It was a valuable antique, probably worth thousands. *But I'll never part with it*, he promised himself, tucking it into his pocket. *And who knows? Maybe, just maybe, it will lead to more time-travelling adventures...*

Suddenly, Tom felt an elbow in his ribs.

"Your go, birthday boy!" his friend Veejay said, thrusting the bowling ball at him.

Tom looked down the lane at the triangle of pins that were waiting for him. Carefully, he took aim and released the ball. It thundered to the end. *BAM!* All ten pins went flying.

"You got a strike!" his friends shouted. "Hooray!"

Tom beamed with delight. His dad put an arm round him and ruffled his hair.

"Well done, son," he said. "I didn't know you were such a crack shot."

Tom looked up at Dad and saw his blue eyes twinkling behind his tortoiseshell glasses.

"Oh, I've been taught by the best," he said, thinking of Isis and grinning.

TIME HUNTERS

TURN THE PAGE TO . . .

➤ Meet the REAL Egyptians!
➤ Find out fantastic FACTS!
➤ Battle with your GAMING CARDS!
➤ And MUCH MORE!

WHO WERE THE MIGHTIEST EGYPTIANS?

King Tutankhamun was a *real* Egyptian Pharoah. Find out more about him and the fearsome Egyptian god, Anubis.

ANUBIS, was the Ancient Egyptian god of the Underworld. He had the head of a jackal and the body of a man. His job was to protect the dead on their journey to the Afterlife, and he was also the god responsible for mummification. He was said to weigh a dead person's heart, to decide whether they had been good enough to enter the Afterlife. A light heart meant that a person was good.

EGYPTIANS
ANUBIS

Brain Power	350
Fear Factor	400
Bravery	360
Weapon: Fear	400

— TOTAL **1510** —

KING TUTANKHAMUN became Pharaoh He was about 9 years old. Because he was young, he had two powerful advisors – General Horemheb and the Vizier Ay. Tutankhamun was about 18 when he died. In 1922, the archaeologist Howard Carter discovered Tutankhamun's tomb in the Valley of the Kings. Most pharaohs' tombs had been raided by thieves, but Tutankhamun's tomb was full of treasures, such as a gold death mask. These treasures have travelled around the world in exhibitions seen by millions of people, making King Tutankhamun the most famous pharaoh of Ancient Egypt!

EGYPTIANS
KING TUT

Brain Power	185
Fear Factor	180
Bravery	205
Weapon: Bow and Arrow	160

— TOTAL **730** —

ISIS AMUN RA was an Egyptian princess, born around 3,000 BC. Her name was inspired by the Ancient Egyptian goddess, Isis. When she was ten, she fell to her death when visiting a new pyramid. Isis is very cheeky and loves to make jokes. Unfortunately, Anubis doesn't find her funny and he trapped her in a statue as punishment for being disrespectful, until Tom freed her. Isis is an excellent archer – a skill she's used many times during her adventures! Although she's a bossy boots, Isis is a loyal friend and she never, ever gives up.

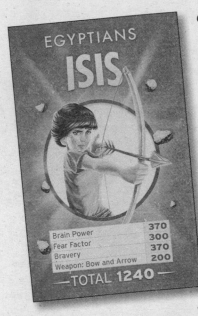

EGYPTIANS

ISIS

Brain Power	370
Fear Factor	300
Bravery	370
Weapon: Bow and Arrow	200

—TOTAL **1240**—

TOM isn't Egyptian but it is in Ancient Egypt that he completes his first quest. Tom was just a normal school boy until he released Isis from the statue and began his adventures travelling through

time. Tom's favourite subject is history and he spends lots of time at the museum where his dad works, so he knows lots about past times. But Tom's not just a history fan — he's also brave on the battlefield and uses his courage and strategies to defeat mighty warriors much bigger and stronger than him.

WEAPONS

Tom and Isis help King Tut to fight against the Hittites, to drive them out of Egypt. Find out what weapons Ancient Egyptian warriors used in battle.

Egyptian chariot: used in battle to charge towards the enemy footsoldiers. The Egyptian soldiers driving the chariot were called charioteers and were usually armed with a bow and arrow or a spear.

Javelin: a sharp metal point attached to a long wooden pole. Javelins would be thrown over long distances to spear the enemy. Javelin points would often be poison-tipped to make them extra deadly.

Bow and arrow: a crucial weapon during battle. Footsoldiers had a lethal aim and would shoot many arrows into the enemy soldiers as they advanced.

Khopesh: a sword with a curved end. Soldiers used it like an axe, slashing at the enemy. The hooked tip was also used to pull shields away from opponents.

ANCIENT EGYPTIAN TIMELINE

In EGYPTIAN CURSE Tom and Isis travel to Ancient Egypt
and meet the famous pharaoh, King Tutankhamun.
Discover more about Ancient Egypt in this brilliant timeline!

3100 BC

North and south
Egypt join together.
Hieroglyphic writing
developed.

1700-1550 BC

The Hkysos tribe invades
Egypt and introduces
the chariot.

2500 BC

The Sphinx and
the Great Pyramid
at Giza are built.

1500 BC

Pyramids
replaced by
tombs in the
Valley of
the Kings.

1332-1323 BC
Tutankhamun
rules Egypt.

330 BC
Alexander the Great
invades Egypt and
founds the city of
Alexandria, home
to the ancient
world's greatest
library.

**1479-1458
BC**
Egypt's
first female
pharaoh,
Hatshepsut,
rules.

664-525 BC
It becomes popular
for Egyptians to
mummify their pets.

31 BC
Queen
Cleopatra
is defeated
by the
Romans.

TIME HUNTERS TIMELINE

Tom and Isis never know where in history they'll go to next!
Check out in what order their adventures *actually* happen.

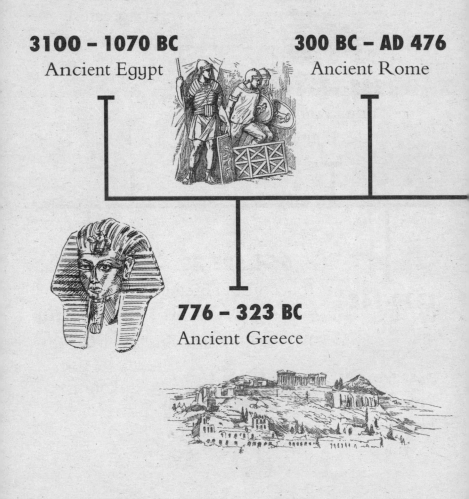

3100 – 1070 BC
Ancient Egypt

300 BC – AD 476
Ancient Rome

776 – 323 BC
Ancient Greece

AD 1000 – 1300
Medieval England

AD 789 – 1066
The Age of the
Vikings

AD 1500 – 1830
Era of piracy in
the Caribbean

FANTASTIC FACTS

**Impress your friends with these facts
about Ancient Egypt.**

➤   Pharaohs didn't wipe
their own bottoms. Instead
they had a royal bottom
wiper to do it for them.
That job stinks!

➤   An Ancient Egyptian cure for blindness
was to mash up a pig's eye, mix it with red
ochre and then pour it
into the patient's ear.
*Good job they couldn't
see what was coming…*

➤ Children in
Egypt didn't wear
any clothes until they
were teenagers as it
was so hot. *Ooo-err!*

➤ Ancient Egyptians would mummify
their dead. To make sure the body didn't
rot they would take out all of the internal
organs, before wrapping
the body in cloth. To
remove the brain they
used a hook to pull it out
through the nose.
That's a big bogey!

WHO IS THE MIGHTIEST?

Collect the Gaming Cards and play!

Battle with a friend to find out which historical hero is the mightiest of them all!

Players: 2
Number of Cards: 4+ each

 Players start with an equal number of cards. Decide which player goes first.

 Player 1: choose a category from your first card (Brain Power, Fear Factor, Bravery or Weapon), and read out the score.

 Player 2: read out the stat from the same category on your first card.

➜ The player with the highest score wins the round, takes their opponent's card and puts it at the back of their own pack.

➜ The winning player then chooses a category from the next card and play continues.

➜ The game continues until one player has won all the cards. The last card played wins the title 'Mightiest hero of them all!'

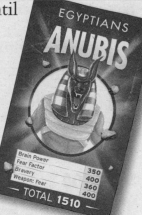

For more fantastic games go to:
www.time-hunters.com

BATTLE THE MIGHTIEST!

Collect a new set of mighty warriors – free in every
Time Hunters book! Have you got them all?

GLADIATORS

- [ ] Hilarus
- [ ] Spartacus
- [ ] Flamma
- [ ] Emperor Commodus

KNIGHTS

- [ ] King Arthur
- [ ] Galahad
- [ ] Lancelot
- [ ] Gawain

VIKINGS

- [ ] Erik the Red
- [ ] Harald Bluetooth
- [ ] Ivar the Boneless
- [ ] Canute the Great

GREEKS

- [ ] Hector
- [ ] Ajax
- [ ] Achilles
- [ ] Odysseus

PIRATES

- [ ] Blackbeard
- [ ] Captain Kidd
- [ ] Henry Morgan
- [ ] Calico Jack

EGYPTIANS

- [ ] Anubis
- [ ] King Tut
- [ ] Isis
- [ ] Tom

THE HUNT CONTINUES...

Travel through time with Tom and Isis as they battle the mightiest warriors of the past, searching for the other five hidden amulets.

Got it! ☐

Got it! ☐

Got it! ☐

Got it!

☐

Got it!

☐

Got it!

☐

Tick off the books as you collect them!

DISCOVER A NEW THRILLING TIME HUNTERS ADVENTURE!

Travel through time with Tom and Zuma
as they search for six gold coins…
Will they find the treasure and win
Zuma's freedom? Find out in:

Got it!
☐

Got it!
☐

Got it!
☐

Got it!
☐

Got it!
☐

Got it!
☐

Who was Marshal Wyatt Earp?
How wild was the Wild West?
And where could you find gold?

Join Tom and his new friend Zuma
on another action-packed
Time Hunters adventure!

"Where are we?" asked Zuma. "And what
are you wearing?" She looked down at her
own outfit. "What am I wearing?"

"They're dungarees," said Tom, brushing off the knees of his sturdy denim trousers. "And I think these checked shirts are made of cotton."

"What about these strange sandals?" Zuma lifted one foot, then the other.

"Not sandals…" Tom corrected her with a grin. "Boots. Cowboy boots!" He reached up and tipped the hat on his head. "And cowboy hats. We've landed in the Wild West!"

"Hmm," said Zuma, looking worried. "Exactly how wild is it?"

"I'm not sure," Tom admitted. "All I know is that in the late 1800s, gold was discovered in America's West. Thousands of people hurried there to try and get rich. That's why they called it the Gold Rush—"

"Babbling!" Zuma cupped her hand to her ear. "I hear babbling."

Tom looked hurt. "Well you did ask…"

"No," said Zuma, patting his shoulder. "I didn't mean you were babbling. I meant I hear running water."

"Let's follow it," said Tom, feeling hopeful. "Maybe it will lead us to a river that rushes with gold, like the riddle says."

With Chilli trotting along beside them, Tom and Zuma found their way to a creek. Then they followed its winding bank through the trees and scrub.

The further they walked, the more the woods thinned. Soon they arrived at the edge of a clearing, where the creek broadened into a wide pool. Standing knee-deep in the rippling water were two boys. The taller one looked like he was in his late teens while the smaller boy was only a bit older than Tom and Zuma.

"What are they doing?" Tom whispered.

"I think they're searching for gold," Zuma explained. They watched the boys dunk shallow pans into the water. Every so often, one of them would let out a joyful 'Woo hoo!'.

"Maybe my gold coin is in that pool!" said Zuma. "Let's go and look, before those boys find it."

She was about to dart into the water when Tom saw something that made him grab Zuma's shirt and pull her back.

From the opposite bank, two men with red handkerchiefs tied over their faces came bounding out of the woods. Before Tom could shout a warning, the men took the boys by surprise. With a sharp blow, they knocked them over and snatched up their entire haul of gold!

TIME HUNTERS

Go to:

www.time-hunters.com

Travel through time and join the hunt for the mightiest heroes and villains of history to win **brilliant prizes!**

For more adventures, awesome card games, competitions and thrilling news, scan this QR code*: